The Witch-Child and the Scarlet Fleet

Mary Catelli

Published by Wizard's Wood Press, 2016.

THE WITCH-CHILD AND THE SCARLET FLEET

First edition. May 8, 2016.

Written by Mary Catelli.

The Witch-Child and the Scarlet Fleet

Sullen gray beneath the leaden sky, the sea swells rolled toward the distant shore. One uncommonly bold flying fish broke the surface, but only one, and no gulls soared. Neither fish nor bird wanted to go near the Scarlet Fleet's port.

No more than he did, thought Alik sourly, and sailed closer. The horizon showed no sign of the port. Even the cliffs were only a dark line on the horizon. They had hours of this yet.

The sail—drab, off-white, brighter than the seascape—swelled from his witch-wind and bore them on. And on. Other pirate strongholds lay near the ship routes they preyed on, but not the Scarlet Fleet, not so long as Habrec the Witch-Prince led them, and bewitched their ships to go wherever he pleased.

"We should have gone the way you came," said Constantine, abruptly, behind him.

The wind tugged at Alik's hair. For a moment, he pondered. Set the boat against the waves the right way, and turn the wind, and he could pitch Constantine overboard. Turning the wind again would ensure that Constantine could not get back aboard before he drowned. Then Alik, alone, could sail off and ignore both the king and the Scarlet Fleet.

Habrec would approve, of the death at any rate. He would have earned his noose, even if the king thought he had perished on the way to the stronghold with Constantine.

Alik turned to face the knight: dark, built like a bear, and glowering at Alik with amber eyes. Hellfire eyes, thought Alik, glaring back. Constantine's gaze shifted sideways as if he eyed at Alik's hair—that moon-blond, witch-child hair—as if he were surprised, and annoyed, that Alik had not dyed it while aboard the boat.

"Couldn't," said Alik. Maybe he would have brought them that way if he could, and maybe not—he sailed at the king's command, not of his own will—but it did not matter. They did not sail on a witch-ship like the Red Hawk.

"Did you try?" said Constantine. "Did they tell you you could not?"

As if the king would have let him take the Red Hawk—as if that would not reveal the falsity of their story.

"We should make haste as it is," said Constantine.

For this voyage to take a year and a day would not be a moment too long for Alik's taste. He turned his attention back to the sail before Constantine could bait him into more speech. If he had known how his moon-blond hair would mark him out in the kingdom, or that Egbert and the other fools on his crew, captured, would denounce the ingrate witch-child who had deserted them, he might never have had the courage to leave the Red Hawk.

But—his hands clenched into fists—that would not have mattered if the king had cared about his innocence, or his life, instead of ordering him back to the port.

A large swell bore the boat up higher. Alik adjusted the witch-wind, to fight less against the waves. He glanced at the cliffs again and thought them the worst possible distance. Far enough to brood before they arrived, but altogether too close.

"I can't speed the boat too swiftly," he said. "Even if I had the magics, I could not betray my knowledge to the pirates. It would imperil my ability to—serve the king."

Let Constantine find a bone to pick in that.

Constantine snorted. "They thought you powerful enough to be useful on a pirate ship."

"But not powerful enough that they feared making me angry." They had feared Hilarion like that—but only if they drove him to the wall, so that if he did not care whether he lived or died. And they knew that Alik could not possibly be so powerful as Hilarion.

His mouth tightened. He had been powerful enough to deal with the pirates, if not the king. Even under Egbert, the Red Hawk might have escaped with the aid of his witchings and gone on a successful raid, to sail back here alive and in triumph, loot-laden. Alik drew his breath in and forced it out again. And having made him a pirate. Earned his noose, as the pirates would say—with admiration, no less—and force gin into his hands to drink to his success.

He eyed the shore again. Cliffs were coming clear, looking less like a line and more of a shape, and even this gray weather could not hide their color. He set the sail again, to bring them closer. This close, Constantine could tell if he dawdled.

And waiting would not make the port more pleasant.

Minutes later, he said, "We're nearly there."

Constantine grunted in surprise. "The cliffs—they're red?"

"As blood," said Alik. "Wasn't until last month that I saw cliffs come in any other color." At least, with his own eyes—images in a scrystone were so small as to look not quite real—but if they sailed for a year, a month, a week, and a day, he would feel not the least desire to tell Constantine his tales.

Constantine snorted. "Red as their sails. Dyed in blood, no doubt."

Alik opened his mouth to deny that—but could he? He eyed the rock again. That the cliffs were red was among his first memories, but the pirates had lived here for many a year before his birth.

The gap that marked the port came clear as a bit of grayness among the red. Alik steered the boat before he concluded—no, the pirates would brag of dyeing the cliffs red. Every night, in their cups, they would brag of it, not caring that every slave in earshot had heard it twenty times, and knew that the pirates who had done the deed had long died. The cliffs had been red before any pirates set up their port here.

He felt half surprised that the pirates did not brag of it anyway, but then, they could only if they had thought of it.

Constantine looked over the waters. Alik set his jaw and sent the boat toward the harbor. A dozen ships (the full dozen!) swung at anchor, their scarlet sails furled. Motley buildings, built of weathered wood, sprawled behind them. A fortress of stone with two towers loomed in the midst of the dingy huts. Nothing green, of course—nothing grew here. The red cliffs lurked behind, half-hidden by the buildings, crumbling in their own time.

That fortress would not loom in the royal city or any other port. He had seen that much. It would look like a commonplace warehouse. As for the rest, they would have clumped about the city gates where the poorest of the poor lived. Which described the slaves well enough, but the pirates lived no better.

He bent his attention to sailing onward, and watching for rocks. The witch-wind slowed under his hand, and the waters calmed as they sailed into the leeway side, and the harbor's shelter.

A shout sounded over the harbor; someone must have sighted them. Crowds gathered and gawked at the boat.

His shoulders set, Alik kept his gaze on the sail. He wished they could have arrived early, in the dawn grayness before the pirates roused from drunken slumbers, while slaves cherished their escape into sleep. If they had stolen ashore, Constantine could have hidden, and Alik claimed magical return. But that would have required another night on the high seas, and risking Constantine's realizing that—and it was too late now. The pirates had weather-witches enough to match against him.

He brought the boat to shore.

Constantine, wretched man, looked unperturbed by the swarm. Starvelings in filthy rags huddled in alleys and odd corners, but pirates and their favorites came as well, their finery ramshackle, ill-fitting, gaudy but clashing, none too clean—they pressed and pushed to stare better, and talked endlessly—though no one spoke to either of them, or loudly enough for them to hear clearly across the water.

And none of them started to fight. That would have been another chance to hide, fights never stayed small, even if he would have had to hide with Constantine.

The boat ground on the sand. Alik let the sails go slack and eased forward in the boat, to scramble out on the sands. Lighter by his weight, the boat rode up in the water, and he tugged it farther ashore. Constantine rose to climb out and heave the much lighter boat entirely ashore. No one, even a slave, came to help—of course.

In the crowd, his lip curled, another wind-witch watched him. Alik let his gaze go on. The wind-witches were no danger. None of them had bothered to learn more than the wind spells, and all had scorned him for his apprenticeship to Hilarion. Other wizards lived in the port—prisoners and slaves, whose spells were useful enough to keep them alive and not powerful enough to allow escape—those wizards might prove a danger to the two of them— but none of them appeared in the crowd.

And Maximus, the only powerful wizard among the pirates' ranks, no more appeared than Habrec himself did.

Constantine gave them all a contemptuous survey, as if wondering why he had chosen to come to this pitiful port.

Two pirates, enveloped by coats too large for them but of peacock-blue brocade, drew close enough to eye Constantine. They talked in low voices. Constantine straightened and stared back as if he had done a menial task in hopes of luring some pirate into treating him as a slave, so that he could teach him his lesson.

One weather-beaten pirate, with gray in his hair, waved at them, his hand already unsteady. His other hand held a bottle of gin, which, from how he hefted it, was already half empty.

"Ho. Come to join us? A short life and a merry one, I warrant you!"

Constantine, coldly, turned those amber eyes on him. The pirate gave him a grin that showed how few teeth he had left, and took another swig of gin before plopping down on the sand.

In the midst of the murmurs, a hoarse voice, barely human, rose. "The king. To the pirate king!"

The cry was taken up, echoing, resounding with cries of "The pirate king! The witch prince! Habrec!"

"Make haste, make haste," one wiry old pirate said. "He will be angry if we keep this from him."

Constantine managed to conceal his flinch well. The crowd surged forward and hustled Alik and Constantine along the stretch of packed red dirt, between decrepit hovels, that passed for a street. Constantine strode with contemptuous ease. Alik scrambled to keep up and thought, sourly, that Constantine had no difficulty passing for a man who wanted to be a pirate.

More and more bystanders pressed about them. Fewer slaves, but more pirates, gaudy in scarlet silk, or purple velvet, or brocade in intricate colors forming dragons or phoenixes.

Several slaves, in this alleyway or that, gaped at him. Some of them, he knew. Alik studied the dirt underfoot. His sober clothes bore neither silk nor velvet, but they were reasonably clean and intact—though he had once been one of their number.

All the more reason to make use of such escape as he had had. Alik straightened. Ahead stood the one well-built building in the port. Built of black stone, looming, the fortress had long made Alik wonder whether it had stood before Habrec sailed the Scarlet Fleet here. They walked toward it. Hilarion had not known of such a fortress or why anyone would build it, but Alik could not imagine either slothful pirates or driven slaves building so well—even if they had bothered to fetch the black stone.

Even in the cloudy day, the fortress cast a shadow over them, and the air, as still in a tomb, felt colder.

At the gates, Habrec's guards, perhaps the only souls in the camp with any discipline, eyed them and listened to the babble.

Then they deigned to let in Alik and Constantine alone, under guard. A few blows from their spears' ends drove back any soul who tried to follow, even one claiming he had brought the twosome here and deserved reward.

Within a few steps, they left behind the light from the doorway.

Lowering though the clouds had been, they had let through more light than shone in here from the torches. Vaulted rooms and hallways rose into gloomy indistinctness. Under them, pirates and their captive playthings swarmed, filling the air with their din. Every now and again, a shrill laugh rose over all. Here silks and velvets bore embroidery in gold and jewels; whenever light struck them, they gleamed as brightly as the eyes, which watched like wolves awaiting the moment to strike.

Even these pirates pulled back, though, from the guards leading Alik and Constantine on and on, by a path Alik had walked only once before. That time, after Hilarion's death from fever but scarcely after his corpse was cold, the pirates had made him weather-witch aboard the Red Hawk.

The air still smelled of smoke, of fine vintages carelessly spilled, of blood. Many pirates had died here when a chance quarrel surged up, with those crowded about as likely to die as those quarreling.

Alik wondered why he had not felt, the last time, how surrounded by weapons he was. He had known they could strike him down on the moment, on a whim, but he had not felt the weapons so.

Constantine showed no sign of noticing.

Music drifted from ahead, muffled by the walls.

One pirate stood, for a minute, before their path. Alik swallowed. This close to the throne room, the pirate had to be a favored captain—and the woman on his arm, lacking the dull eyes of most captives, looked avidly at them, as if she wondered whether the captain's largesse extended to prisoners. Her dress carried so much lace that Alik could not see the color of it, only that much of the lace had been torn off other clothing to be tacked on in a mismatched array.

He looked back as steadily as he could. Constantine, no doubt, looked unworried and as if carved from granite—he did not dare look aside to see that expression—and the guards moved forward.

With a grunt, the captain turned aside. The woman's mouth pursed, but she went with him. With them gone from the path, the throne room lay clear, even here visible through the arch. The guards moved them forward, inside.

Alik could not compare its size to that of the king's. This windowless room, lit only by torches, was cavernous with shadows. But though the walls lacked the pale smoothness of marble, and the gleaming windows, the pirates gathered about in finery more glittering than the king's courtiers had, however often in mismatched colors or in disarray.

They left the center of throne room open, though.

The gilded throne, catching the torchlight, stood on a dais opposite the door. On the black flagstones before it, a woman danced. Her jewel-bright skirts flared like a flower's petals, in shades of violet, sapphire, and scarlet.

And on the throne sat Habrec. The Witch-Prince, the Pirate King, the master of the witchery that sent their ships across seas without sailing on them and gave the Scarlet Fleet its power and its terror-inspiring fame. Bigger than Constantine, lowering like a bear, dark, bearing a sword that could easily slice Alik in half, he watched the dancer through eyes narrowed to slits.

The guards stopped in the doorway, and not in order to send the two of them ahead.

Alik glanced sideways from the throne. The jester, simple, or frightened to simpleness by his capture, mumbled over his bauble. His bag of tricks lay at his feet with its welter of oddments, bearing slight enchantments to amuse. Alik's tongue touched his lips. He could not make out the musicians. Fortunate musicians.

Alik looked back to the throne. The jester would not perform until Habrec dealt with a stranger and a wayward wind-witch who arrived by boat. Though as the music went on, and on, Alik wondered whether that was because the dance would last long enough to unnerve them.

The woman swirled, colors flaring. Alik fought down fidgets but could not wrestle down his thoughts. They stood in a pirate stronghold, he had deserted a pirate ship, all its pirates had died on the gallows, Constantine was a knight in the king's service. . . .

Alik forced his breath in and out. Habrec was not some madman. All the captives had been captured in raids on towns and cities, or ships foolish enough to fight or flee. Merchant ships that cut their colors on the sight of a ship from the Scarlet Fleet lost only what the pirates craved from their cargo, not their passengers, not their sailors. Habrec, pragmatic soul, had enforced that rule with executions and liberated captives taken from ships, to preserve and keep strong the fleet, and it lasted so well that he had never had to either execute or liberate in Alik's lifetime.

But he remembered the tale of a ship that the pirates had thought carried gold. Finding only pale gray ingots, they had cursed them as tin and thrown overboard a king's ransom in silver.

A pirate bellowed for wine, and a slave scurried with the jug, to pour with her head bent low, trying to avoid notice.

He should stop acting as if he had not seen the throne room many times before, if only once by this route. Constantine had not shuddered—he glanced sideways and saw the tension in the knight. He glanced away before the knowledge could infect him with more terror.

The music stopped.

The woman sank in a curtsey deeper than any woman had given the king, glided off the floor, and sat in a corner, her eyes downcast.

For a long minute, Habrec did not stir, his gaze still on the floor where the dancer had stood. Then, he looked up. Slowly, his gaze crossed the distance between them. He looked over Constantine with a leisure that Constantine's stubborn expression did not perturb. Then his gaze settled on Alik as if eying every inch answered all his questions, and not one answer pleased him.

Finally, he looked at the guard. His voice was a thunderous growl. "There had better be a good reason for you intruding on— amusements not meant for your ilk."

"News from the Red Hawk, my lord," said the guard.

Habrec shook his head. "Not news. News only if that witch-child finds his tongue and tells the truth. I know I did not send some starched paladin with him. I wonder whether he really is old enough to win his noose."

Words surged to Alik's mouth. Even knowing Habrec baiting him, as he baited many another in this hall, he had to fight to hold them back. A pirate duel would end him. The king's plans could roll on without him; Constantine would not intervene on his behalf.

Habrec's lip curled. "A bookish little witch-child. I should have known Hilarion would make you as useless as he was."

Laughter prowled about the court.

Though Hilarion had taught Alik from every book he could lay his hands on—begged, borrowed, or lying about unheeded—he had also taught him how to act in a pirate king's court, etiquette taught in no book. Habrec had given him no orders. Alik stood as still as he could.

"Come." Habrec straightened. Alik walked forward. Constantine calmly followed, as if the center of the throne room were not the hardest place to defend, and the best lit, leaving all his foes in shadow. The air, laden with the smell of smoke, stood perfectly still about him. Alik felt like a candle flame, tossed by drafts, unable to keep steady a moment, and in danger of being blown out.

Habrec drew his sword. It gleamed like ice as he brought it down, its tip pointing inches from Alik's feet.

"Speak, witch-child." His deep voice grew more menacing, like the advance of a towering thunderhead. "Tell me of the Red Hawk. Tell me of the ship I placed you on, to win your noose."

His court was, for once, silent. Not even the slave children's footfalls sounded. Alik felt as mute as any of them, but all was lost if he kept silent.

"It foundered, Your Majesty." With a little well-placed help from a little wind-witch—but Alik kept his voice level. "The captain and crew alike foundered it." True enough. If they had not insisted that wind-witchery do all the work, if they had acted as sailors, he would never have had his chance. At the time, he had grown dizzy with joy. "They were caught and hanged by the neck until dead. Their bodies still hang from the gallows."

Not even the last drew a murmur from the crowd.

"Waste of a good ship." Alik shrugged. "Should I have wasted a wind-witch, trying to rescue them? As if I could—I can not witch such an escape." He raised his head to meet Habrec's gaze. "But I escaped, with some aid, and brought a warrior to add to your numbers, one not so worthless as the crew of the Red Hawk." To add a traitor and spy to your numbers—but Habrec hardly desired his advice.

Habrec snorted. "Still the bookish little mouse that Hilarion taught." A low rumble of mirth came from the crowd. Habrec sat back. "But you have served me well enough."

It felt as if the flagstones had vanished underfoot. The room was silent again. Alik did not move; he did not breathe; he only waited for Habrec to spring his trap.

"Another task I have for you, since you serve me. Kill me this companion of yours."

Alik started and stared at Habrec. Even Habrec's presence could not hold back the guttural laughter, all about the room.

"Your Majesty, he helped me—"

Habrec sneered. "So he could become a pirate, not out of his tender heart. And you owe him for that? More than you owe the

Witch Prince who holds the freedom of the seas for the Scarlet Fleet?" He lowered his voice. "The Witch Prince who gives you another chance to earn your noose, and win a short life but a merry one?"

He produced a knife like a conjuror's trick; one moment, it was just there, in his hand: a long jagged knife with, Alik guessed, a handle of bone.

He hurled it, and it clattered on the floor at Alik's feet.

Alik drew a deep breath. In, out. In, out. Then he knelt to take the knife up. The handle was, indeed, bone, and felt cool under his fingers.

A statue could not have stood more still than Constantine. From his face, he might have been struck deaf when Habrec spoke, and so be ignorant of the order. Until Alik, turning, met his hellfire eyes and saw the flicker of contempt in them. He thought—and King Petros would think—it was Alik's duty to kill him and preserve his ability to spy—as Habrec thought it was his duty to kill aboard the Red Hawk.

At the moment, if he had known a spell to blast every living thing in the world, he would have cast it.

With the knife in hand, he rose. A ball fell from the jester's hand, and Alik's eyes narrowed.

"So slow," drawled Habrec. "So reluctant."

"To botch it before the Pirate King?" said Alik, glad of an excuse to face the throne rather than Constantine. "A wind-witch is not a master of blades, and I should not leave him floundering in his own blood like a landed fish, so that another has to finish him off." He shrugged. He felt light-headed and wondered if he had gone mad. "Unless you gave me the knife as a sign I should witch him to death."

Habrec snorted as if conceding a point. "As if you could kill a man with light and wind, little witch-child—but you know enough of a blade."

Alik nodded. He noted in his mind where Constantine stood, a little behind him. "Quite enough. For this."

The knife flew through the air, before him. Roars of fury rose. Poison-green witchfire flared about Habrec, ready to ward the blade off.

The knife flashed past the throne, like a hawk seeing nothing but its prey, and tore into the jester's bag of tricks.

For a moment, in the startled silence, Alik thought it all in vain. He had missed any enchantment that would have mattered, and doomed them both.

Then the bag burst from the magics inside. Lights in gold and white and blue fountained out, drowning out the witchfire and filling the air to the roof with their brilliance. Even having turned his face away, Alik was blinded. But ready.

He surged back to Constantine. Grabbing his arm, he said, "With me."

Not a moment too soon. Uproar echoed throughout the hall, drowning anything he could say, but Alik drew Constantine off with him, to the wall behind the throne. Screams punctuated the clamor—screams, mostly, of "I'll kill him!" Alik fumbled with his free hand, knowing where it was but not where he was.

The wall yielded to emptiness, so abruptly that Alik staggered into it. Then he fled, giving his eyes, and Constantine's, no time to adjust to the gloom.

At least Constantine had followed without question. The pirates would rage to kill. Likely, they struck about the throne room already and killed some of their own number. Escape was possible only before the spells ended, and the pirates could see, and see how many they had killed, and swear revenge on him for that as well.

And Hilarion had made him memorize the way—

The window slits, high up on the way, gave him light enough for him to see his still too dark path, before he realized what his memory meant. He stopped.

Constantine bumped into him, hard enough to knock him a step forward. His words pushed out past his teeth, in a barely intelligible snarl. "What fool thing now, witch-child?"

The first place they would seek him was Hilarion's old hut. He forced his breath out. Constantine glared at him. No longer too surprised to do anything but obey, but he still did not know the ways. He had to use Alik as his guide, even if Alik did not know the ways perfectly.

Which, Alik thought, would be wise to keep from Constantine.

"This way," he said—down another slave corridor, which at least the pirates would not know. It led to a door strange to him. Opening it revealed a narrow passageway between ramshackle huts. Unlike the street, most huts lacked doors to it, and it was far narrower. He could not tell which one it was, but he would know soon enough.

Constantine eyed it and said nothing, but followed. After a minute, Alik held up his hand to stop him. Clamor burst out next to them, pirates swarming from the fortress and tumultuous noises reaching through the thin walls. He could hear nothing clearly of what they said, but he could almost see the torches and weapons.

They had feared to make Hilarion desperate, had even let him die of his illness before they claimed his apprentice. They should have feared the same of him. Though—Alik's mouth twitched—none of them perhaps had realized that it would make him desperate, that order.

Hilarion would have approved, he thought, despite the danger.

He glanced sideways. Constantine at least had the wit to stand still despite the ruckus.

Someone bellowed, demanding to know what was going on. The footsteps did not move as far as the shouting rose. Jeers rose, that only fools would let captives escape, and then the sound of blows. Even a Pirate-King could bring only so much order to pirates. Smiling a little, Alik hurried along again, while the hunt turned into a brawl.

The slave alleyways interlaced throughout the huts and hovels of the port, with walls to shield them from the pirates. He scurried through them like a pale little mouse, eying the path ahead. The slaves had to be cowering away from the rage, but the corridors had gaps, so that slaves about their tasks could slip in and out, and there they could be seen. Each time he came to one, they flitted across with extra care, and Alik breathed a sigh of relief every time they were not seen. After half a dozen, he thought the pirates must have gone to see the ruckus. They had best use the time wisely, before Habrec enforced his will—the noise of the shouting and fighting was not far behind them—but Constantine, even if a large, dark mouse, was as silent as he was. Alik led on.

One relieved moment, he realized for certain where he was, and started their path, out of the central buildings, toward the half-empty ones. Constantine eyed the tumble-down shacks but said nothing. Alik kept an ear cocked to the ruckus. The noise did not seem to spread—it even seemed to die down—but the pirates would be quieter as they stopped fighting and started searching. He could not keep his breath from coming light and fast. If he escaped this port alive, he would delight in having defied Habrec as no one else had ever dared.

If.

Finally, they reached a plunder house. Not where the pirates stored food or rope or water, or anything else useful, but fripperies that had caught no pirate's fancy, and that they had not needed to trade. Alik slid through the door.

Only the daylight that slithered through cracks where its boards were ill fit together gave the place any light, and sounds from outside were muffled. Dust like a veil of years lay over every crate and bale. Pirates had made slaves build new shelters for their loot, and slaves had not raided for anything here.

Alik sighed, turning his face away. Useless enough that they might hide safely here.

Constantine's hands clamped around his throat, and he squeaked—the noise cut off as Constantine's grip tightened.

In a rage-laden growl, Constantine said, "*What* did you—" The words cut off as if Constantine was being choked, and Alik, futilely, kicked. He had no chance of landing a good blow, but Constantine hurled him down, knocking him against a crate.

Alik lay against it, breathing hard. He would have bruises where he struck the wood as well as on his throat. If, that was, Constantine did not finish what he had begun.

Constantine stood in the largest clear space on the floor, breathing hard, engulfed in shadow. Alik could not see his face in the gloom, but his hands formed fists and released them, again and again, and he fought to steady his breath.

Finally he spoke, forcing out every word. "What fool thing did you think you were doing?"

Alik drew a deep breath. "Saving your life."

"So it means nothing to you," said Constantine. "The dead children—the ruination—the horrors they inflict when next they assail a city—you wandered through a city and saw all that would die when they attack—"

Alik let his breath out. As if Constantine's purpose here were not to keep him as the king's spy.

"Finish it, then," he said, curtly. "No matter you might, with my aid, still carry out the king's command." He turned his back to Constantine and pushed off the ground—his arms ached—to stare into the massed crates. And wait.

His heart beat out the moments too fast for him to judge time by them. And how long should he wait? They could not stand here forever, but Constantine would not speak.

Finally, he looked over his shoulder. Constantine glared so banefully at him that Alik thought only the lack of words poisonous enough kept him silent.

Constantine's gaze shifted up to meet Alik's. He grated out each word. "You didn't even know those spells would work like that."

"Where did you imagine the jester got them?" said Alik.

Constantine's voice softened not at all. "What do you intend to do now?"

Alik swallowed, making the bruises ache. "Sneak. The port has a maze of alleys all about, so slaves can sneak, unnoticed."

Constantine snorted. "I wouldn't think pirates would care."

"They don't like the riff-raff getting underfoot."

Constantine's hand swept the air, dismissing. "Enough to build these ways?"

"Pirates?" said Alik. "Build? Anything? Stab a slave for a glance at a favorite, or no reason at all, yes, but *build*?" He looked about. "Or even store things away—I doubt any pirate can tell what clothes they have here." He glanced at Constantine. He had, after all, started this to save Constantine's life; he might as well carry on. "You'll have to skulk. Unless you want to try to swagger off as a pirate. Or pass as ill."

Constantine snorted. "*Ill.*"

Alik tilted back his head to meet his gaze. "I dare say Rosalba— she's a herbwoman—could whip up a posset to have you coughing and feeble, if you want the risk of dying for their sport. As you stand now, when any pirate sees you—a man like you is a pirate, or kept in chains if he's skilled enough to keep alive—and you're no blacksmith, or rope-maker, or wizard, or doctor."

"You should have thought that before you started this." Constantine's lip curled. "I suppose they still think you a child."

"They're like you. I'm man enough to sail as a pirate, and man enough to hang for it. But other than that—" Alik turned to the crates. Not, of course, tightly nailed up. Pirates had torn them open to see the loot. Even when nails had been restored, the planks were loose, and he could strew the clothes he did not need all about.

"They leave these things hanging about?" said Constantine, his lip curling. "So much for a short life and a merry one—they could trade this loot for more revelry."

"Point of pride," said Alik, prying open another crate. "Sometimes they trade, if they are short on rope or the like, but they say that with the Witch-Prince's magic sending them to where they can strike best—" The plank leapt free, making him stagger. "—they can hardly *need* to sell it." He tossed the plank aside. "A few more raids would cover it. They have to direct them, sometimes, to get food and water, and even—" He seized another plank. "Even raid land for food. But *trade*? No, they leave the loot for foolish slaves if they want it."

It took some minutes to find the best crate, but that one revealed clothing too drab to catch the pirates' gaze. Alik sorted out some shabby, ill-fitting clothes, dragging it out to the best light to be sure of the colors. It would not offend the pirates, prone to stabbing slaves for taking clothes the pirates had not wanted, but it was neither tattered nor stained with reddish dust. Yet. He doubted the dust would take an hour, and they could never be clearly seen. Pirates would see who they were before they missed the tatters.

He carefully pulled out a hood for himself. Dingy blue, but the color hardly mattered. He could not let a pirate see his eyes, either, but the hair they could see from a distance, and it would be as distinctive and betraying here as in the kingdom.

About changing, at least, Constantine did not argue. As he straightened his new ash-brown tunic, he said, "How safe are we in the slave passages?"

"Slaves may rat us out." Alik transferred his own knife to the new clothing. "Not many. Not from loyalty, but only a fool would expect a reward." His mouth twisted. "Still, we are not short on fools. And some will be just too afraid to not tell, unless they fear us more."

"Domenic," said Constantine, without looking at Alik. "Domenic may live yet—not having been shackled to such *help* as you." He swept a loose mantle about himself. It at least swathed if it did not hide his weaponry. It might work at a distance.

Alik nodded and turned to leave. With only one doorway, this building was no place to be caught. Even a wizard could see that. His mouth set. And they did have to find Domenic, and act against the pirates, who would hunt them down in time.

He still did not know how he managed to walk briskly down the corridors again, until they came within earshot, and walked as softly as little mice again.

Voices were still clamorous, outside, but nowhere near as loud as before. By one doorway, making out laughter, Alik stopped and held out his hand, flat, before Constantine. They stood there, Alik scarcely breathing.

The pirates roared with mirth over what fools the captains looked like, running all about after Alik vanished—carried himself off to the kingdom again, he gave it away when he talked about escape spells—nah, if Hilarion could have taught him he would have escaped himself—but Alik could have stolen a spell book for his studies since then, it took him long enough to return—and Alik crept onward, despite the risk, knowing the pirates would not leave.

The pirates argued on, whether he had turned invisible and sat in the great hall, pilfering jewels and fine wine. That, they thought most likely. Why else would he have returned?

The voices faded behind, and Alik's mouth twisted. No mention of Constantine—Alik wondered whether they knew he existed. Rumor could have left him out as too dull to discuss.

He ducked into a roofed alley. From the gaps in the wall, light splattered on other side, beige spots on dull brown wood, like a dreary, captive wildcat.

"Spy holes," said Alik, softly. "We're on a hillside—you can see the square below."

Constantine eyed the holes. And why not? thought Alik. The biggest square, where they divided loot, and fought duels, and drank to drunken slumber—where was more likely to hold Domenic?

Outside, the clouds had thinned enough to show watery sunlight. An enormous pile of wood sat in the square. Pirates gathered around, glancing often at a doorway, and some talked of how long it would take.

"Ho!" someone shouted. Pirates—Alik scowled, but he could clearly see them—pirates themselves lugged their burden, with others cheering their efforts on.

A boat, Alik realized.

Not just any old boat, but the one he and Constantine had arrived on. The pirates hefted it onto the bonfire wood to merry cheers.

Alik forced his breath in and out. It was, indeed, any old boat, chosen for its ordinariness. The magic to bring them here had been Alik's own, the pirates had boats like it, boats that the two of them could steal in the end, but Alik felt like a prisoner seeing the key to his cell being destroyed.

A pirate brought the burning torch to the wood. For a moment, smoke emerged, and nothing more, as if the wood stifled the torch. Then flames leapt up and licked the driftwood. They blossomed orange, with shots of blue or purple running through them, and grew toward the boat. The fire crackled and sent fountains of sparks into the air.

Constantine's hand rested on his shoulder. "Best time to move. That will distract them."

Alik nodded, but said, "I can do better." He held out his hand and readied the spell. Nothing more than amusing trick, usually but—his eyes narrowed, as he invoked the words.

The flames on the boat shot up a pure snow-white. Alik took only a moment to relish the horrified expressions before he followed Constantine. They would take it for something in the driftwood, or the boat, but it would hold them.

Indeed, voices already demanded that some wizard explain what enchantment the boat had held. And why he had not seen it first.

The alleyway held rickety stairs, leading downward over a slope. Alik drew a deep breath. Here, the alleyways would be more heavily traveled; the one down the stairs was the worst, lying between the ale barrels and the pirates' revels. They needed every scrap of wariness they could muster.

Something flitted through the air—bird-like, glinting golden when stray light fell on it—and toward them. Alik's heart drummed almost before he realized what it was. He had only seen them once, he had been too young to understand much then, but the mere sight brought back terror and memories of sudden blood.

"Kill it?" whispered Constantine.

Alik nodded.

Constantine's sword whispered out. As the shape flew closer and grew more clearly hawk-like, he lunged. The sword bit between wing and body. The thing fell into a clutter of metallic feathers—all feathers, apparently, except for its sharp beak and claws, which twitched on the dusty floor.

Grim-faced, Constantine struck again. Feathers flew and lay still.

His mouth dry, his heart only slowly quieting, Alik dropped to one knee. The pirates might not chase them, but Habrec had others to aid him. A wizard like Hilarion might win some respect from pirates for fear of what he might do if desperate. A wizard like Maximus, who held respect and received his share of the loot, had to please the pirates to hold that place.

Alik poked through the ruined bird, and his back prickled with the knowledge that another bird could fly toward him at any time. Still—

His mouth dry, he said, "It's not very good. He has nothing of yours or mine to strengthen it." He swept up the shattered bits, to hide them. "But I know Maximus. He won't send only one, because he can send a whole cast of them. Force of numbers will take us down in time." He drew a deep breath and straightened before glancing about the ways, remembering. "We have to stop them at the source."

Constantine snorted. "You think Habrec won't notice the death of a pet wizard?"

"No. He wouldn't." Alik set out briskly, down a new corridor. "At most he would notice the lack of spells, and in his rage, he might learn of the death—but since we will not kill him, it does not matter."

At least, this path took them by uncommon ways, and they could move with haste.

Constantine strode after without more questions. He did not put up his sword. Another gleam in the dark shadows had him striking again. Alik gathered up the feathers—these ways were not so little used that they could leave a trail—and Constantine stood watch over him.

"How long?" he said, glowering, as Alik straightened. "Do we chase about this port for hours on end?"

"Not much farther," said Alik. Unable to take themselves off into towers, wizards lived at the edge of the port—though not so far off they had to fear escaped slaves. Which meant the two of them had nearly reached it.

He turned his gaze back on their path, and his eyes narrowed. Just as well. Maximus would have gone slowly at first, but the birds would multiply swiftly once he had refined the spell. After a moment, he ran. When Constantine smashed a third bird against the wall, Alik ran on without breaking stride. Cleaning up the bird later would have to be enough. They could not be caught standing over it.

The floor turned into a ledge, with a short stair leading down from it. Opposite stood a building—sturdier than a hut, with rooms and windows. Alik jumped. He landed, with a jolt, before an arched doorway, filled with shadow.

Not too many shadows—they did not hide the bowl, larger than a ship's wheel, glittering with a golden liquid that rose almost to its brim. Mist rose from it in pale coils, as if from the sea on a cool evening, but mist should not twist around, take on bird-like form and solidity, and dart toward them.

Constantine's sword flashed out, striking it down. Alik drew a deep breath and wove his sealing spell. Another hawk had almost formed as he reached the end. Two more were forming.

The last word slid out, and he squeaked, "Fall back!"

For a fearful moment, he thought Constantine would not listen. Then, he inched away, his gaze on the birds. They took on fuller form and snapped at the air with strong jaws. Alik's heart beat out the moments—

"Faster!" he said.

Constantine swore, but leapt back. His foot caught on the uneven floor, and he stumbled, falling to one knee. A golden hawk plunged to the attack. Alik's knife sliced through the air, pinning the creature to the wooden wall.

Behind it, a swarm of golden hawks splattered against the seal. They snapped and struggled but did not cry out. Alik's mouth twisted. Even Maximus, monumentally self-absorbed, would have had a hard time avoiding the racket if they screamed—no doubt the reason for their silence.

He let his breath out and rubbed the back of his neck. The other good fortune was that Maximus was too proud of his hawks, and too absorbed in his studies, to come and check.

Alik retrieved his knife. He hoped that there was not too much more luck ahead. If he exhausted his good fortune in the first hours in this port, he would die soon. They still faced the pirates, and whatever other witchery Maximus or some other wizard could cook up, and any runaway slaves sulking in shadows and stealing what they could.

He put up the knife. Not to mention that Constantine already had little inclination to listen to him. He collected the dead birds, and turned to climb the stairs. They still needed to gather the other one, and then it might be wiser to take a roundabout route to other places where they might glimpse Domenic—

"How long will *this* last?" Constantine's voice was heavy on the air.

Alik hesitated and racked his memories for how the moon had been when they set sail. The last measly scarp of a crescent—"Two days." He turned on the steps. "The *spell* would last much, much, much longer, but even Maximus will have to notice it when he leaves, at the first crescent. He'd hide in his hole forever, if he could but—" Alik shrugged. Maximus would come out to strengthen some spells, the price of Habrec's favor, but all Constantine needed to know was the time. "In two days, we have time to do things."

Constantine snorted, putting up his sword, and walking toward the stairs. "We'll see. If Domenic has not done better than we have, we may do nothing."

Alik shrugged again. "We have to act quickly, whatever happens. Habrec will not keep the ships here forever."

That silenced Constantine.

Alik led the way back to the last bird, which he gathered up with care. He crouched over where it had laid a minute longer, considering which path to take now.

"We came that way," said Constantine, his voice harsh.

Alik straightened up. "Did you see Domenic in the crowds?"

After a moment, Constantine shook his head. "I looked," he admitted. His face was half shadowed.

The daylight was fading under clouds again, Alik noted; they would have to return to the torch-lit parts before they were lost in gloom.

"We will cast about for other places where they often gather. By routes that the slaves are less prone to take." He glanced at his hand. "We can throw these aside in a back corner where no one will look, while we are at it."

And I know the route better if we go another way. He tried to push that thought away—and then to distract himself by picking out the way and heading off.

Several huts stood to the side of Maximus's, farther apart than most. They crumbled into dust. No one wanted to move into a wizard's home after his death—even the wretched hut of a feeble wizard, who could not escape pirates and eked out a living with tricks for pirates and even slaves. Alik's brooding gaze moved over them. Maximus would say that they were even too feeble to win Habrec's regard. Alik's eyes narrowed; then, he had heard the tales of how Maximus had groveled and begged and promised anything for his position. Hilarion, he knew, had not.

His gaze moved ahead, as if drawn by a lodestone. His feet moved more slowly. He would hate seeing it, but by this path, he had to. His free hand clenched into a fist.

Hilarion's hut showed no outward signs of ruin, but its door swung open. He peeked inside. Enough gray daylight seeped in to show that the hut had been stripped bare, of everything from Hilarion's scrystone to the beds and cooking pots. His fist tightened. His mother's hut had been stripped at her death, he had been lucky that Hilarion had taken him in, but he had not seen this; they had snatched him to be a weather-witch almost before he finished burying Hilarion.

They would laugh and tell him to be grateful that they allowed the burial.

"That one's barely damaged," said Constantine. "Best place to hide the birds—"

"No," said Alik so abruptly that Constantine blinked. But he did not owe the knight an explanation of his life. "The next one will be better." He walked briskly to it and told himself that some foolish soul might hope that not everything of Hilarion's had vanished, and visit the hut. It took him only a minute to throw the feathers into a corner. He drew a deep breath and went to lead the way back into the heart of the port. Down dusty alleyways—he had lived in this red dust all his life, but now, after only weeks away, it bore down on him.

He let his breath out very slowly. He might escape it yet.

Down a few rows of huts, he hesitated, hearing footsteps ahead. He drew Constantine to a corner.

Constantine scowled. "This won't hide—"

Alik shook his head and gave him a sharp glance. And cast his spell. Shadows gathered round, making the very air murky. For them, thought Alik, nothing more than murk, but at least Constantine held his tongue.

The slave, a boy with a bruised face, scurried along without a glance at their corner.

Alik released the spell. "That only works for a place," he told Constantine. "And not well if we move, even in it."

Still scowling, Constantine nodded, and they stole along alleyways. Footsteps had them hid in odd corners, sometimes with shadows. Through spy holes, or the cracks that slipshod building had often left, they eyed the pirates as they fought and drank, and roared tales of real or imaginary fights and treasure hauls. Alik remembered the art of darting across streets where pirates fared without being noticed. Perhaps he was even too cautious there, but for now, at least, they had time for safety.

Perhaps. The endless array of pirates and slaves and favorites exhausted him. Could they search all the port in two days? Some pirates were new—some slave boys sent to earn their noose after he left, but others taken off ships, and he had no notion whether he could recognize this Dominic.

And it could happen that Dominic could not help them at all.

He trudged on. The passing of hours meant they could check every place twice, and still miss Dominic, what with all the movement among them. Even the gray daylight started to slacken as they searched on.

Then Constantine, peering from the shadows by a doorway, pointed. A man, as dark and bear-like as Constantine, leaned on a table over his ale. He sat back, unsteadily. His clothing looked drabber than most pirates', though he wore a sky-blue vest and a flame red sash across it. The colors clashed.

Another pirate shouted for Domenic to come. He lifted his head.

"Huh. I'll stay with—" He raised his mug. "Good ale."

Constantine's voice, low by his ears, said, "Wiser than you in evading what he does not wish to do."

Alik drew his breath in and forced it out again. Slugging Constantine would do him little injury and would draw eyes. Nevertheless, his fingers curled together, and then after he had forced them apart, curled again.

"How do we get about, behind him?" Constantine pointed at the wall behind Domenic.

Alik walked off, picking the way, wary of slaves bearing ale. The walls here were more ramshackle than usual, where slaves had need to spy; when he glanced out a crack between planks, Domenic no longer sat where he had. Alik swallowed but walked on, hoping for revelations.

"There you are." The voice was clear, sober, and recognizable. Alik stopped.

Without faltering, Constantine pushed by him and clapped Domenic on the shoulder. His voice was low but amused. "Amethyst still working well, I see."

Domenic nodded. Not so tall as Constantine, broader in the shoulder—plus the finery, which made it easy to distinguish.

"If," said Domenic, "we had aimed to cause uproar among the pirates, I would say you had succeeded beyond the king's dreams."

Constantine rolled his eyes. "There is no need to remind me. This, for my sins, is Alik."

Domenic inspected him. For a moment, Alik studied the beaten earth; then, feeling defiant, he straightened and met Domenic's gaze. Let Domenic see how moon-pale he was—down to the pale gray eyes, and the even paler eyelashes.

Domenic's eyes were dark, unreadable. After a minute, he snorted. "Watch how you stare—even in the slaves' alleys. I saw you."

Alik forced his breath out.

"Have you learned anything?" said Constantine.

Domenic nodded. "Habrec's going to raid another city. He's chosen a city, he's drawn up his orders—and not for a chest of medicines, this time."

Alik flinched. Neither knight seemed to notice.

"He's sealed them in the Tower of Winds. But I can't stagger there under the pretense of drunkenness. Even in the slaves' alleys." He snorted. "Especially in the slaves' alleys."

"I've been there," said Alik, surly. When Domenic looked at him, he glared back.

"What do you want?" said Domenic.

"To be very far from here. You know how I was sent." His eyes narrowed. "I am not here of my own will."

Domenic snorted again. "There is no place far enough for you to have no fear of the Scarlet Fleet."

"Am I the only person that's true for?"

Constantine, cutting in like a sword blow, said, "Does Habrec venture to the Tower of Winds by evening?"

Domenic scowled.

"No," said Alik. "Habrec doesn't get so drunk as the rest, but he spends the nights like any pirate." He glanced up, past the tower and the cliffs. The clouds had thinned farther, to show that the sky had turned flaming red and pink. About the port, pirates had lit torches, here and there. Orange light blazed on walls and cast dark shadows, but it would seep into the back alleys as they went. Enough to walk by, if they took care.

"We had best be off," said Constantine. "To find it in the hours before they start to rouse again in the morning—and *you* have to go back to drinking."

Domenic cocked an eyebrow but left. After a few strides, he staggered into the torchlight. Alik looked away. For all the books, for all the scenes Hilarion had shown him in his crystal, he had never seen knights as such actors—though if they acted well, he would not have known they were knights.

And Constantine's glare was no act.

Alik walked along the alleyway, pondering that both knights had offered to come here at the king's command. Though *they* had chosen the king's service.

After some minutes, with sounds fading behind them, Alik said, "We're taking the back route. It will be full night by the time we get there, but fewer slaves, that way."

Constantine muttered, "Some sense anyway."

How flattering, Alik thought, and prowled on. They circled around. The alleyways, though still beaten earth, had loose dust over their way. Their footprints only added to the scuffle, reminding Alik they were not the only ones who needed to pass with as few eyes to watch as they could wrangle.

The gloom thickened. Little even of the torchlight reached to alleys, but enough to see their way. At one corner, Constantine turned to survey the light rising over the walls.

"Waste of torches," he said.

"They'll just steal more," said Alik. "No pirate urges another not to waste, well, anything—it shows a want of faith in their skills—if they're really short of a thing they do a raid to go after it—and what if they all died tomorrow? Then it would really go to waste—and what's the point of a short life and a merry one if it's not merry?"

His voice echoed oddly from the walls about them. A light gleamed ahead—more evident from the shadows it cast than the light itself. Alik put a finger to his mouth. Constantine scowled, but as long as he was silent—

Alik crept closer. Maundering, nonsensical words, rambling tunelessly on, reached them. The growing light—grayish like dawn—made Constantine's set face all the clearer. The alleyway reached a barren room, marked only with dust. Gray light suffused it. On the beaten earth, an aged man, little more than skin and bones, sat and stared, maundering on.

Alik laid a hand on Constantine's arm and drew him around, behind the motionless man. The danger of his seeing them was little, but enough to be wary of, when it cost them nothing to avoid it. Constantine looked about as if seeking where the light came from, but he did not speak until they slid down the alleyway on the other side, and the walls hid them from the man.

There, his gaze shifted back. His voice was low. "Who was that?"

Alik kept his voice as low. "A captive wizard. Some, like Maximus, throw themselves into winning the pirates' favor with crafty spells. Some—" Like Hilarion, he thought. "—survive by trading little magics with slaves and pirates. And some—" His hand swept the air to take in the door. "—go mad."

"And some become wind-witches."

"Oh, no. That *honor* is reserved for those born here. Who had nowhere else to flee." Alik walked on. The gray light faded, leaving only torchlight.

At the next turn, Constantine's hand brushed his shoulder. His voice was softer than before. "Followed."

Alik saw nothing, but pointed to a corner. There, he gathered shadows about them both.

A youth appeared. Torchlight glittered on a knife in his hand, though from his dress he was a slave—Alik's gaze went to his face, and he stiffened. A nut-brown, square-faced youth, a little older and taller than him, and more solidly built.

Ivo.

Alik's gaze went back to the knife. Not just the blade glittered. The hilt had gleaming jewels, and Alik thought he recognized it. Pointing, he mouthed to Constantine—magic.

Constantine did not look concerned, and Alik felt no surprise.

Ivo continued toward them, unrelenting. His gaze was so steady that Alik realized that Ivo did not look at the corner, or even at them both, but at him. Constantine tensed beside him.

Alik dropped the shadows. "It's me. You don't need the knife."

Ivo started and did not move forward. "It's you I'm looking for. You could not witch yourself away." His voice dripped poison. "Who else would I look for? After the uproar you made? After I was your *student*?"

"I taught you a trick or two," said Alik. "In exchange for a few goods."

"You were my teacher," spat Ivo. He shifted as if to flank him. Alik turned to face the other youth. Constantine moved, but Alik could not turn his attention aside from Ivo.

"If I were your teacher," said Alik, "you would have to obey me." Only the knife's glitter kept him from laughter at the thought of Ivo's obeying anyone who could not force him.

Ivo laughed, shortly, muttered, and threw the torch into the air. It hung there, casting orange light and vast shadows, as Ivo turned back to Alik.

"After your treachery? After you fled the Red Hawk? Every wizardling in the port would cut off his hand for that chance! You can not even *bother* trying to win your noose."

Blame Hilarion, Alik thought, glancing at the knife for only a moment before looking back to Ivo's face. He was my teacher, I obeyed him, and he used his scrystone to show me, again and again, places that I could escape to.

He said, "You would think worse of that ship if you served on it."

Ivo's lip curled. "Heh. And *you* think you taught me all I know." He lunged.

His knife clattered against Constantine's sword.

Ivo looked up at the knight with no fear in his face. "So loyal," he whispered, "to *die* for him." He lifted his dagger toward his mouth, close enough that he could have kissed the pommel, and whispered, "Alik."

Constantine's left hand seized Alik and shoved him behind. His sword almost glowed from the light it caught as he pressed the attack, and steel clashed. Ivo scrambled back, and Constantine stopped, eying him warily, as if Ivo could flank him to get to Alik.

Alik grimaced. Wise, perhaps—he could not match Ivo with even ordinary blades.

Ivo's gaze met Constantine's and flickered away from those hellfire eyes. "You're a big one. What's your name?"

"Habrec," said Alik.

Ivo drew up the dagger toward his mouth again. Then he stopped and glared. Constantine's mouth twitched, and Ivo snarled and lunged again, with such furor that he almost made Constantine's greater reach and skill moot. Alik stepped back as blades furiously thrust and parried, and racked his mind for any wizardry that could aid. A light spell, even if he could cast one swiftly enough, would blind all three of them—as bad for flight as for fighting—and draw the pirates, eager for a hunt. They would laugh as loudly at the fool pirates who thought Alik had fled. . . .

Constantine's sword lashed out. Blood marred its edge and seeped from Ivo's arm.

Ivo snarled. "The two of you against the one of me." The gemstones glittered redly. Ivo looked thoughtful, his eyes narrowed.

Alik thought of a spell. As quick as he could, fighting to shift the air just so, he made a voice right by the hilt of Ivo's knife.

It whispered, "Ivo."

Ivo froze, staring at the knife as if Alik had transformed it into a snake. The hilt shifted in his hand, cutting, drawing blood. Ivo's mouth opened to scream.

Constantine's sword sliced through the air into Ivo's throat. Blood fountained, and the only cry to escape was a gurgle.

The blow had not cut Ivo's head off, but it landed at an improbable angle to the rest of his body, and even by torchlight Alik could see how the blood had darkened toward crimson. He stood very still and gulped as he tried to subdue his stomach. His empty stomach had no business heaving up, to burn his mouth, and he could not take his gaze from the widening pool of blood.

"Well done," said Constantine, going to clean his sword. "This time."

The knife glittered on the ground, despite the blood. Alik dropped to one knee to put his hand over it. The motion took his gaze from the body. He drew in quick sharp breaths and cast the shield spell, warding it from touch. Here he did not even have to worry about the knife pushing against it. Then he wrapped shadow about it, rendering it an undistinguishable lump.

Drawing a deep breath, he stood. He managed to keep his back to the body.

Constantine studied the dust. "We'd best be gone. No one heard us—" Obviously, Alik thought. "—but this is too traveled. Someone may notice, and try to curry favor."

Alik shook his head. "We'd best hide the body."

Constantine cocked an eyebrow, looking at the pool of blood.

Alik swallowed. He had done it before. He had even known the names of some slaves he had done it on. The one spell he had mastered by rote—the one spell that many a slave knew.

"You don't imagine—" His voice dripped scorn as he stood over the puddle. "—that pirates will let us be, when they trip over bodies or slip in the blood?"

He dropped to one knee again to incant the spell. The flesh was colder already, and the words sour and bitter in his mouth, but Ivo's blood flowed steadily, deep red, into the dust, which drank it up.

The ground still bore blood stains, but in the red dust, a man would have to look with care to see them, and nothing about this place would catch the eye for that. Alik stood. And bloodstains alone would not betray them, not in this port.

Constantine, impassive, swept the corpse to his shoulder. His gaze was steady on Alik. Alik reached up to snatch the torch from the air, and quenched its flames. Then, after a moment, he led Constantine back, not quite along the path they had taken. With the gray light reappearing, he pondered what room was best.

Then he heard the silence. After a frozen moment, he inched forward.

The wizard lay in a pool of his own blood. Alik stepped forward, staring. Who—why would even a pirate stab a harmless old madman? After having tolerantly let him live for so many years? Some even thought that harming him was bad luck.

Constantine eyed the wound. "The same blade. Or one much like it—but it looks like he tracked us through this place."

Alik swallowed, hard.

Constantine closed his eyes for a minute. Then he asked, "Do you want to hide this body, too?"

Alik shook his head. "Nothing to connect him to us." He wished his voice was not so thin.

Constantine nodded, contemplating the body again.

Praying? wondered Alik, and said, sharply, "We have to go. This was no tragedy to him."

"That's a tragedy in itself," said Constantine, almost gently.

"There." Alik jabbed his finger, pointing into one alley and a dark doorway there, to a musty room, laden with boxes and crates years ago and undisturbed since. Perhaps since before he had been born—or Ivo had been. Alik shuddered.

Constantine stirred up dust, until he laid the body behind some crates. As good a hiding place as any, and with the dust disturbed, he left no clear path to it. He paused a moment.

Alik scowled. "He hated me, because he *wanted* a chance to earn his noose."

Constantine straightened, his face muffled by the shadows. "He earned it. And more besides. You could have—"

"No, I could not," said Alik. "Many a witch-child has earned a noose even younger than I." If he had realized that early enough, he would have refused to learn the wind-witching. Or at least have tried to refuse. Hilarion might have insisted, for protection, since he had cared whether Alik lived or died.

He glared at Constantine.

Constantine glanced at the body again. "He said—but he is no witch-child—"

"What?" said Alik. "You don't believe that superstition, do you? A witch-child has to study like everyone else."

A bell's heavy note rang over them. Constantine looked sharply about. Alik's stomach curdled.

It rang again.

"A ship's returned," said Alik, sourly. Constantine would profit from the knowledge. "Come."

He picked his path. Soon, as the bell tolled yet again, they descended a side stair. Not to a particularly useful location for any other purpose, but gaps in the wall let them see the sea swells, touched by starlight and glancing torchlight, without so much as a flying fish rising above the waters.

The bell tolled, and the Tower of the Stone blazed with light. Blinking a moment let Alik see the light pouring from the height of it, in blue and white and green beams, making the waves glisten, flooding the port with light and shadow, even sketching out the last scraps of cloud.

He could not make out much of the tower. Hilarion had always told him that it worked like a scrystone, but Alik had never seen how Hilarion had ever gotten close enough to tell.

The light beams twisted in air. Out of the brilliance, a ship sailed. Under the green light, the sails looked black; under the blue, a ghastly dark purple; but the white showed them scarlet. The ship sailed toward the docks.

Alik's mouth twisted. Especially when no scrystone did anything like that, and if one could have, Hilarion would have fled long before he took Alik on as a student.

The pirates swarmed toward the docks, calling to their fellows, hearing their returning cries. The ship tied up, they turned to the loot. Slaves, dragged from the buildings to the dock, or dragged, battered and beaten, from below the ship's deck, were burdened with great chests—many of them—but some chests two or three pirates took up. Alik's breath hissed out. That could not be good, loot that pirates did not entrust to slaves' hands.

Pirates, and staggering slaves, started the torch-lit procession through the port, to flaunt the treasure. The torchlight flared over the walls as they vanished among the buildings, and cast enormous shadows, distorted images of loot-bearing figures, against the cliffs.

Alik let his breath out. The pirates would pile it in great heaps and rejoice over it, but that would also mean they swarmed over the port in their celebrations.

He glanced at Constantine. "We should go. Now." He did not have much hope, but they set out through the alleyways by yet another path—to hear the pirates' uproarious glee.

He still hoped, a little, but casting about soon showed that pirates, rejoicing, had indeed crossed every path in the port, cutting off every way to the Tower of Winds.

And their bragging revealed that the ship had taken cannons and shot. They would be well-armed for their next raid on a city— and the Witch Prince already made the plans for that.

When Alik turned to Constantine, all the play of light from the moving torches could not hide his set expression.

The words felt flat in Alik's mouth. "We can't get in. We have to wait for morning."

Constantine's expression hardened to steel. For a moment, Alik thought he would refuse with no heed to the revelers about, who would kill them both as part of their amusements.

His voice was curt and low. "Where can we sleep?"

"A storeroom. We can find something."

Constantine nodded. His mouth twisted. "We've done so already. Twice."

Alik led him off, this time more slowly. This close to the Tower of the Winds and their stone stronghold, the pirates thronged, whooping down this alleyway and that one. Once, as a procession of torches passed where Alik and Constantine crouched in shadow, Alik's eyes closed for a moment. If they just rested here, they would be closer, come morning.

Constantine poked him in the side.

Alik shifted his weight. The pirates had gone far enough away. He drew closer to the doorway, ready to dart over to the next slave alley.

A small boy, his eyes bruised with exhaustion, lugged a flagon far too large for him out of the alley. Alik's heart beat out the moments before they stole across, but they needed to move. The light from the stone illuminated their way, but it would not last forever, and then they would see no more than by torchlight.

In the next square, pirates argued. Not over loot, surprisingly this close to a return, but Alik did not linger to listen.

A dog barked, and Alik stopped. Slowly, he turned his head. Two pirates led out four dogs: great hunting hounds, one white as bone, one black as soot, one red as blood, and one green as grass growing on ruins where once a city had stood, before the pirates came. The dogs, tugging at their leashes, growled and snapped. Alik glanced at the pirates holding them. He did not recognize one, but the other was Fedor, who grinned, baring his teeth.

"Let Habrec muck about with cannon all he likes," Fedor bellowed. "He lets spies run about our stronghold—"

"They fled," shouted one pirate. With a mug of ale in hand, he slouched against the wall, and he sounded resentful of being roused.

"If that bratling could flee," said Fedor with a sneer, "he would have fled years ago and taken Hilarion with him. He knows a jester's tricks with light and color, and Habrec was a fool not to see that was the spell before the—throne."

Some pirates muttered about the stone, but Fedor looked at his hounds.

"These beauties will hunt them down and show him. They must have turned invisible."

Alik wondered whether Fedor had found anything to give them the scent. Biting his lip, ignoring a sideways glance from Constantine, he lifted his hands for the spell and sent a breeze across the way, wafting his own scent before the beasts.

The blood-red hound bayed, deep in its chest. Alik worried his lip. If it lost the scent, the hound would cast about, searching—he sent the breeze off, toward the doorway. The other hounds bayed, and joined in the chase.

Alik started off along the way. Someone might hear the footsteps, a slave might come along, but the hounds were more dangerous than either circumstance. He glanced into the room at every chink, and sent the breeze on.

Constantine shadowed him, silently. He could only hope that the knight had guessed at his spellcraft; he could not add a voice to the noise they already made.

"There, that does it," said Fedor, full of malice.

Alik drew a deep breath and sent the breeze down a roundabout route. He scampered for the room it would eventually lead to. He had won himself a moment, with the shorter path, but he wrestled with ways to get the hounds off their track. Spices, he thought. Conjured rightly, they would work as well on the hounds as the jester's lights had on the throne room. But for it, he needed to find spices, and fresh ones as well.

He reached the room, and found it filled with pirates swilling fine wines—the ship must have borne more than weapons—and jeering at Fedor's folly.

Alik's eyes narrowed. For a moment, he thought of Habrec, but in this uproar, the throne room would be worse than the Tower of Winds. He had to act quickly. He stopped, his breath so harsh he half-thought the pirates would hear it, but they did not turn. In the middle of this crew stood Captain Ogier, his mouth twisted by the livid scar across his cheek—the scar that new slaves were warned marked out his cruelty, even among pirates.

The hounds' baying grew louder, as they raced about the loop and closer once again.

"Fedor's little toys." Ogier swilled more wine. A scrawny girl, dead eyed, came over with the flagon of wine. The hounds bayed again, Ogier jerked the tankard, and the wine slopped. The girl's eyes widened—perhaps the first feeling she had shown in months—and Ogier backhanded her, sending wine over the floor like blood and throwing her into the wall.

The pirates roared with mirth. Ogier grinned. Then he shivered. Alik's mouth twisted into a smile; he increased the breeze, letting it play over Ogier.

The hounds, baying, burst into the room, their eyes brilliantly avid, their mouths lolling open, their legs moving with grace and speed, until the blood-red one, in the lead, leapt on Ogier. Blood splattered, invisible on it, but vivid on the other three as they pounced, maws biting and splattering themselves with more scarlet.

Shouts of outrage rose. Some scrambled to haul the dogs off Ogier. Others, more prudently, drew blades to stab the beasts, or went to club them. Fedor stared from the doorway as if wondering what Ogier had done, when a pirate struck him with a meaty fist, and Fedor's followers surged into the fight.

Alik, his breath steadying, half-wished to stay and see if Ogier died, if Fedor was killed, but he turned his face away. Constantine showed no more approval than a stone. They picked their way out, along corridors, and the sound of fighting followed. Once or twice, Alik glimpsed a pirate stabbing another, neither man having been among the crowd where the fight started, but he had seen too many brawls to hope it did much damage. More than once, he hid them in shadows from slaves, who scurried by faster than usual, their eyes enormous. Alik wondered if they would see anyone in their fright. He looked at the floor as footsteps scurried off. He supposed a city looked worse like after a raid.

"This way," he said, thinly. Constantine, mute, his expression impervious, followed. Alik tried not to think on how—even not counting the dead from the brawl—he had already killed more men than Habrec and Constantine had wanted him to. His jaw set. At least, more than they had wanted him to, then. Who knows how many would have died at his hand by now if he had returned to Habrec's service?

Another musty, out-of-the-way room—Alik wondered, as he never had before, how much of their plunder the pirates tossed aside. He dropped to the floor, not caring much. The light from the stone was fading; it was well that they wanted only to sleep.

"Here." Constantine thrust something before him. His nose recognized it: bread and dried meat. Constantine held an open bag, the same bag they had eaten from during the day.

Constantine snorted and sat himself. "Your pirates aren't the only ones with wizardry. Now, eat."

Slowly, Alik's hands went up to take it. When he bit off a mouthful of bread, it was rough on his tongue, and he felt ravenous. He bolted both so swiftly that he barely tasted either.

Constantine, not half done with his meal, snorted and handed him a water bottle. It held sweeter water than that from barrels. Alik drank and drank.

"Your pirate king is not popular among the pirates," said Constantine. The light from the stone, fading but not gone, played over his face and cast white bars and dark shadows across it. He took another bite of bread.

Alik snorted and felt water slip from his mouth onto his face. He lowered the bottle.

Constantine went on. "So why do they not gut him and get themselves another? A short life and a merry one—they'd be merrier without him."

"The stone." Alik held out the bottle, and Constantine took it back. "The World's Ways. Where would they be without his mastery of it?" He smiled, spreading his hand.

But the World's Ways could not be hard to master. Habrec had done it, when he knew no other magic. To be sure, nonetheless, the pirates had grumbled but never even tried to overthrow him. He rubbed his eyes. He needed rest.

"Get some sleep, Alik. Unless you do not wish to be up with the dawn."

Alik forced his breath out. For all that he had seen and endured growing up, he would not sleep, not so soon after those hounds nearly hunted them down. And the pirates' revelries, or fights, still sounded in the night, louder than most nights. More men would die there. His mouth tightened. He could hope they were all men who had earned their noose—which, he had to concede, Constantine had not. He glanced at the knight, whose face he could not read. Hilarion would approve of his having saved his life, he thought. He sighed as softly as he could. How could he sleep when such thoughts turned in his head?

Still, he lay on the earth, using his arm for a pillow, and closed his eyes. He could rest if he could not sleep.

He felt Constantine's hand on his shoulder—a moment later, it seemed, but gray morning light seeped into the room and made it look still dingier. Even the ruddy shade of the dust could not brighten it, and the still air was bitterly cold.

He staggered to his feet, stretching his arms against the stiffness. Constantine handed him more bread, this time with dried fruit. Alik ate, not quite so fiercely, but quickly. Morning meant slaves moving about, eager to do what they could before the pirates roused. Earlier might have been better, but there would have been slaves, even then.

He brushed off the crumbs and led the way through the dawn.

The pirates had settled down to drinking, eventually. Many sprawled across the streets, often with mug still in hand.

"They must get drenched when it rains," said Constantine, his voice low.

Alik glanced up. The sky still held clouds, if not the blanket of the day before. Hilarion, on days like this, would marvel about those clouds.

"It never rains. Not here. That is why nothing green grows." He walked on, swiftly, picking their way far more directly than he had dared by night.

Even the corpses did not make him flinch. Though the thought ran around his head that there must have been more. These dead could only be those that died so late that the pirates had not cared about tripping over them. After the brawl over the hounds, they would have bellowed for the slaves to haul the dead away.

Some of these might even have died from cracking their heads, falling over while dead drunk. His hand formed a fist. They could not all have died in the brawl he set off.

Constantine glanced sideways at him after another pool of blood.

"I wonder how many will hang for killing," said Alik.

Constantine raised an eyebrow.

"Part of the law. Brawling's all right, but you've got to duel in order to kill—at least, to kill pirates. And—" He shrugged. "They've all earned their nooses."

Constantine grunted. "Unless they claim that all who fought the dead men also died."

"Likely," Alik admitted. In an empty street, he glanced at the Tower of Winds. It loomed, but the spells on it were nothing like those on the Tower of the Stone.

It even had slave stairs, which was its greatest weakness.

Constantine looked about at the dingy buildings in the gray light. Alik chanted the unlocking spells. Long ago, a wizard had sagely feared what would happen if he did not arrive swiftly enough, and slaves had passed the knowledge on, year by year, without—Alik opened the door and gestured to Constantine, who followed him in—without Habrec even wondering why he could bellow for wine and have it in moments.

Or so he had heard. He closed the door and let his eyes adjust. The light was less here than anywhere else but the corridors at night. Alik looked up the stairway. Narrow and plain, of course. Such dust as there was lay, ruddy, in odd corners. Being Hilarion's student might have kept him from servant duties and from being stabbed by some drunken oaf, but it had also kept him from here.

They didn't have time for him to let Constantine know of his ignorance. He strode to the stairs and climbed. Light mounted, steadily, almost with each stair, until they reached the first platform. The tower still went up, but Habrec's chambers were here, where he did not have to continue to climb. Alik put his hand to the door. Not like the Tower of Stone where secrecy was that much more valued.

The door opened easily, to a back corridor, but already he could see astrolabes, maps, sextants, compasses, and other things that Hilarion's teaching had not included.

None of which mattered. Alik strode in and looked about. Habrec had had it furnished with cabinets and desks and chairs, all of fine wood, polished to a mirror's surface; even if none of it matched, none had been damaged by its capture. Papers lay everywhere. And piles of books—Hilarion had taught him using every book he could lay his hands on and had not gotten a third of one of those piles.

They couldn't all be about navigation, Alik thought.

Constantine appraised the room. "How does Habrec give orders to his captains?"

Alik blinked, casting back his memory. He had never come this close, and Hilarion had never dared scry too closely, but he had seen them set out. "Boxes. Wooden boxes, metal bound."

Constantine nodded, looking satisfied. "Thought these looked familiar." He walked over to the stacked boxes in one corner, and Alik felt a fool.

"There's the free life for you—getting your orders in a box just like you were a captain in the navy." Constantine snorted. "Down to the same boxes."

He sounded as if he knew it all before this, thought Alik, bitterly. He looked over and was glad he had not said that aloud. The box still bore the royal crest, even if the metal had dulled with time.

"Dare say that he thinks the rings necessary—" Constantine put his hand to the crest. Alik could not quite follow what he did, but the box slid open, soundlessly. Constantine let out his breath, and Alik edged over to see the paper inside. Constantine took it out and straightened it to read the orders to attack Kingsport.

Alik listened for a minute, but Constantine added nothing more, and he did not suddenly realize that he had misheard him.

"So that's it, then," said Alik.

Constantine nodded, and scowled at the smudges of red dust on the letter and inside the box.

"Oh, put it back," said Alik, "but don't close it."

Constantine eyed him but obeyed. Alik raised his hand and incanted. A whisper of air slid over the letter, picking up dust. Constantine slid shut the box, and the air whispered over it as well. Alik slowly backed toward the slave stairs, letting the breeze catch every fleck of dust. Constantine, warily, eying the dust, edged past him.

Alik closed the door with the dust on his side. Then he swept it to one corner, to hide among the shadows and the other dust. The slaves might not betray them, but best to not give them the chance.

He let his breath out and listened. Outside, nothing more stirred than had before their venture. A grin plastered itself to his face, and Alik forced himself to remember they had to both get away uncaught and get the word out. Their knowledge did the king, and Kingsport, no good. Habrec perhaps had never learned of the stairs, because no slave had ventured to futilely steal from him by the stairs, when there was nowhere to flee with the gains. Even they had work ahead of them.

But Constantine knew that they had only gained the knowledge because of him.

Quiet as mice—down the stairs, out the door, through the alleyways—they went. Slaves hurried about, and even some pirates moved, stirring and moaning, and cursing the drink and the fool slave who had needed a good thrashing.

Already the bodies were gone, and the blood conjured into the dust to make it all the more red.

That thought took the edge of his elation, but no more than the edge. They stole onward, through hovels even more decrepit than those they had used the day before, and out, onto the rocky shore, where jagged rocks hid them from the docks. Alik drew in a deep breath of the salt air, blowing inland, smelling of nothing but the sea. The sky turned from gray to shades of eggshell white and yellow as day approached.

"Here?" said Constantine.

Alik nodded. Constantine surveyed the stones and walked over to the narrowest place leading to the shore. There he drew his sword.

"You won't be able to buy me time enough, if they find us," said Alik.

"That would depend on how far you had gotten in the spell by that time," said Constantine, coldly.

Alik looked away. He felt the heat in his face, and he knew the red would be brilliant. Keeping his back to Constantine, he began the spell. Hilarion had not known it, and the royal wizard had all but taught him by rote. And to get even a single word over land and sea to echo in a far distant room—he concentrated.

When the final words of the incantation slipped from his mouth, there was an expectant pause, the air seeming to stand still about him.

Alik said, "Kingsport," and the air seemed to shudder and, after a moment, let the breeze in again. The spell had finished.

He looked about. Without his noticing, the colors of dawn had given way to plain daylight. He grinned. It had, after all, been little more difficult than hiding that dagger, he thought merrily. Constantine looked up. Feeling light-headed, Alik pondered what to do next. If they sneaked onto the attacking fleet, they could escape the port entirely.

Constantine put up his sword before leading the way back among the buildings. The walls cut off the sea breeze, leaving them trapped in dusty air, though the daylight still brightly lit the way. Alik trailed after, knowing they had no need for haste. They walked on, as the sun slowly rose to shine through the thin clouds over the alleys, and Alik noted that Constantine had mastered the path.

The towers grew clearer ahead of them, they drew nearer to where people lived, and the morning roused yet more. Alik pondered the next days. Looking for a way to escape. No doubt the king had better things for his knights to do than linger in a pirate port after discovering what they had come for.

Unless. He blinked, remembering. He wondered how long Domenic had stayed here, with no chance of escape. If the king tried to press him into staying as a spy forever. . . .

His mouth set. If the royal forces did enough damage to the pirates, they would be able to leave freely.

Then he remembered the hawks.

His mouth twisted. Even Constantine would have to concede that if they could, they should flee rather than die uselessly under Maximus's spell, but the hawks were a greater danger than Constantine, or the king's orders. It did make escape rather urgent.

But they were near enough to the center of the stronghold that he did not dare just speak to him. He crept closer, but Constantine still walked briskly, and there was no time to draw him aside.

Shouts and whoops rose ahead of them, raucous—cruel. Alik grimaced, wondering who had fallen afoul of the pirates. When Constantine scowled and walked toward the noise, Alik followed. Slaves scurrying away sent them into corners behind the shadows, but then Constantine walked on, and Alik wondered when to broach the matter. They were unlikely to have a better chance. If the uproar spread far enough, if it distracted the pirates enough to let them steal a boat, they might escape.

Perhaps even with Domenic.

The bellow came from a square before. Constantine stopped in the slave alley. Alik caught up and froze. Constantine looked so horrified that Alik was afraid to look. He muttered the shadow spell about them and still did not turn.

The pirates' shouts rose, and slowly, as if dragged by a thread of curiosity, Alik turned toward the gap to peer out.

Boden stood there, towering over those about. Boden, Habrec's witless right hand, violent, enchanted, enormous. And before him, sword in hand, Domenic stood, looking ready to fight to the death and full aware that the death would be his.

Alik felt sick to his stomach. Boden did not run free, not here, not in the pirates' stronghold. Stupidly loyal, he did only what Habrec told him to do.

Boden's heavy club came down, knocking Domenic flat.

"Ho! What happens?" Habrec strode in, scowling.

"No kill!" said Boden, pointing.

Habrec snorted. "So *some* pirates can obey their laws." He stood over Domenic, who shifted a little and then lay still. Alik, swallowing, realized that the knight could not rise.

Habrec's voice lowered. "I, however, am King of the Pirates. I can kill. It is my duty to kill, in chains, those who break the pirates' laws."

A murmur went about the pirates—none too loudly, as no man wanted to offend the master of the Ways of the World.

Habrec crouched by Domenic. "And since I have detected a whisper spell coming from these parts, I have set a spell to ensure that no such spell goes out again. And—I have changed my mind!"

He stood then, looking about the assembled pirates. "Ready yourself, men! We go to lay waste the city of Fairington!"

Pirates roared approval. Alik felt the blood seeping from his face. Slowly, feeling he moved like an ancient man, he turned to face Constantine.

Constantine could look even more horrified than when he saw Domenic's plight. Alik swallowed.

Pirates surged forward to haul Domenic up. Domenic did not scream, and if he groaned, the uproar overwhelmed the sound, but his face contorted.

Alik and Constantine scuttled away like mice, but mice would never have had his spell ready to hide them in shadows—forever, thought Alik. Futilely, because those hawks would hunt them out soon enough.

He did not know why, but he scuttled about the alleyways until they could look over the sea. The chains hung there, not empty, even now. A woman's body slumped against the stone. The dancer, Alik realized, and wondered how she had offended, or even if she had.

Futile, he thought, turning his face away. Madness. Though they lurked in shadow, he should never have come here and risked the danger. Even with the hawks lurking, waiting only for the moment that Maximus realized how Alik had stopped them.

But he did not pull back.

Pirates hauled Domenic out. He had more bloodstains and bruises than when they had carried him off, they had stripped off his brightly colored clothing, and they reached for the chains. One taunt reached over the waters: they had even brought him female companionship.

Constantine's hand touched his shoulder. Constantine nodded along the alleyway, and Alik mutely followed.

"He won't last long in that condition," said Constantine, grimly.

"Habrec will have a wizard heal him," said Alik. "It's the only time a slave can get healed." The time that Habrec had besieged a city, only to lift it in return for a chest of medicines—it had been for pirates. He had understood little of the attack and the demand, but he remembered the long hours of his mother's babbling in fever and finally going still.

When they stopped in a dust-laden alleyway, the heat was mounting. Alik dropped to the ground, sitting with his legs bent under him and his head bowed. The hotter it was, the sooner Domenic would die. If Habrec had always known who Domenic was, they had been played for fools. If meeting with them had revealed him—Alik's mouth tightened in a spasm—he had killed yet another man. More than Habrec had demanded of him. . . .

Constantine came up beside him, with water.

Alik drank.

Constantine said, "It's only one knight you've saved."

"Saved?" snapped Alik. "Have you forgotten the hawks and my spell on them? I haven't *saved* you. It will not last because—"

It felt as if someone had opened a window in a dark room—a sudden illumination, so brilliant that he forgot Constantine entirely and stared into air.

Then he closed his mouth and stood. His legs felt stiff already, but he said, "I know what we must do."

"Go outside your Witch-Prince's spell to cast another whisper spell?" Constantine's voice was dry.

"Maximus would have his hawks on us before we crossed half the distance. No, we must do—something else."

Explaining that the spells Maximus used could be twisted would take too long, even if the knight believed him. He had not even explained how Maximus enchanted the tower with the World's Ways in it, to keep people out, and this would take even longer. He looked up at Constantine and set his jaw.

Constantine glared at him. "Is that something else stand here until we rot?"

Alik shrugged and turned aside, calculating. Sunlight shone down the alleyway. No longer gray with dawn, but it would be hours before it turned orange with evening. They would sit about for hours somewhere, and it would be best for that place to be as close as he could get it. Arriving late would ruin all.

"We have to go." But he stood a moment longer, his eyes closed, as he traced out in his mind the route to Maximus's chambers—the best route, not the fastest. The thing they needed least was prying eyes, and they did not, yet, lack time.

He opened his eyes again. Constantine looked angry enough to strike him.

"To save Domenic, no doubt." Acid dripped from his voice.

"Men," said Alik, "have died in the chains in less time than this will take—but maybe."

Despite the rising heat, he set out briskly. His stomach roiled. Actually putting his plan into words would make its absurdity all too plain.

He remembered the hawks. The two of them would be lucky if the hawks only tore them apart—if the hawks caught them. He walked on.

And on. At times, he wondered whether he had taken a too safe route, especially when Constantine had them stop to eat.

They had hours, but stealing about the stronghold could take hours.

Then a slave hurried down the corridor, and his heart hammering, he hid himself and Constantine in shadows. More and more as they drew nearer.

But even hiding from slaves, they eased down the alleyways away from the pirates. As they reached their object, shadows slanted over the alleyways, but the sky was still blue, and the sunlight golden, laden with dust motes—not even orange—with afternoon.

"Maximus's chambers," said Alik, his voice low. "He will emerge soon—"

Constantine snorted. "And you want him to set no hawks on us."

"Among other things," said Alik. "First that—"

He froze, but it was too late. Fool, fool, fool, he had let his plan fill his thoughts, had trusted in how little the slaves came here, and now a girl-slave studied them in the shadows of alley. She—of course—held the tray that would slide into Maximus's room without disturbing him until he wished to eat, and Alik felt the bitter taste of his failure.

She glided forward, not taking her gaze from them. Younger even than he was, and a bruise lay across her face, marked by a heavy hand.

When she came even with them, she met Alik's gaze for a moment and turned her gaze back to the alleyway.

She was out of sight when Alik managed to whisper, "This way." His heart beat—not faster, but harder. He had been saved from his own folly once. He could not even think of risking such danger again. They slid down the last of the alleys with feet as soft as shadows'.

He had known the shield had not failed—the hawks would have descended in moments—but seeing a hopeless jumble of metallic feathers still calmed his heart. They did not rise up so high that he could not, once he got close, see how they trailed back to the bowl. Alik let out a sigh of relief. Only one thing to deal with, then. Maximus, absorbed in his studies, would not have time to restore this spell before he restored the other.

"There," he said, pointing to beside the door. "You will stand there, and I will shadow you. It will not last once you strike, so you must make your blow count."

Constantine studied him for a silent minute. "And you?"

"I will not shadow myself. It will have to be you who strikes."

"What fool plan are you working?"

"One that will not work if you are not shadowed and ready to strike," said Alik. He surprised himself, with how tart he could make the words. "Or if he hears voices here, to warn him."

Constantine scowled but obeyed, and Alik shadowed him. He stepped back, breathing a sigh of relief. He could have explained on the way, but he had this dread that if he did, Constantine would see what a foolish plan it was, and forbid it. At least with the jester's tricks, he had known the spells. This turned on the hope that he could master Maximus's spells quickly.

It was a foolish plan, and Constantine might well reject it. Even without a wiser one.

Alik turned. Constantine could not see the sky from the shadows of the arched doorway. Even if he could, he would not know what to look for. Unless he remembered, from the earlier day, Alik had said that Maximus needed to cast a spell with the new moon.

Alik walked about, looking, until he found a gap in the buildings that let him watch both the western sky and the doorway. He glanced back and forth, moving little more than Constantine did, as the sunlight grew orange, and then the sky took on color in bands: rose, orange, yellow, all of them in hazy shades. And then, just above them in the hazy blue, a narrow scrap of moon, colored golden in the sunset.

A bell chimed within, and Alik winced. Of course. Maximus leave his books long enough to see whether the new crescent moon had risen? Of course he had set a spell to keep watch for him.

He turned from the sunset. He scarcely dared to breathe. If this went awry, they, and Domenic, and all at Fairington, would die.

His breath eased out. Except for the unlucky at Fairington. So it must not go awry.

A shadowy figure shuffled out, as if too stiff from sitting to move freely. Alik thought he heard mumbling, but not enough to be sure of it, even when straining to hear. Light sifted in on the figure, revealing that his hair was dark gray and his robes parchment white, and that he held something in his hand. Alik bit his lip.

A startled cry announced that he had seen the bowl, and the birds. Alik drew a deep breath, stepped forward, and threw another shield spell, to encircle Maximus.

For long minutes, Maximus only poked at the birds, paying neither Alik nor his shield any heed. Alik waited, his hands forming fists that he released as soon as he noticed, his heart hammering out the moments, until, finally, Maximus looked up. His gaze reached Alik, and he stood, blinking like a day-blinded owlet.

Then he drew a sharp breath. "Hilarion's brat!"

Alik bowed.

"Making trouble—what does Hilarion want, this time?"

Alik blinked. He had not dreamed that Maximus's studies could keep him from knowing that Hilarion was dead, and he wondered what Hilarion had done last time, but—

"What a fool you are!" It surprised Alik, how he could make his voice ring. "You can't take your nose from your books long enough to learn that I sailed as a wind-witch—and on so shoddy a ship that I came back to defy the Witch-Prince to his face!"

"Witch-Prince?" Maximus's lip curled. "The fool has half a spell, and that one's useless without that great gaudy stone of his!"

Two, at least, though Alik, and then forced his attention back.

"Impudent brats who think him a wizard are—" He raised a hand. Alik braced himself, and Maximus's mouth shifted into something like a smile. "No threat at all."

Flame gushed from his hand, burst against the shield, and flooded back. A moment, Maximus stood, looking bewildered and even a little singed.

He broke the spell before it harmed him much, Alik reminded himself. He could not expect Maximus to destroy himself so easily.

"As opposed," Alik said, "to a wizard who has to cast his spell by the light of the new moon—to use its waxing to fortify his meager spellcraft!"

"As opposed—" Maximus put his hands out, and his words cut off. Alik fought to keep his face mask-like, as if he did not know the nature of the spell he had cast.

But Maximus hesitated too long. Every moment gave the wizard time to think, and so a chance to realize.

"As opposed," said Alik, "to a wizard who let a mere boy trap him! It's not just this way—I have encircled you, held you entirely—"

Maximus cackled. Alik felt his face contort and was shocked by the horror and fear he actually felt. If things went wrong here—

"Such a foolish pup!" Maximus pushed out with his hands, ready to show Alik that any shield of his could easily be broken out of, from within, by main force.

Alik's heart beat out the moments.

Maximus burst through the shield and staggered into the corridor. Constantine's sword swept through the air. Maximus's throat, completely unguarded, parted before its edge, and blood fountained, brilliantly red even in the gloom.

Maximus's face showed not even surprise as his head tumbled over the earth, spewing a trail of blood.

His stomach roiling, Alik dived to snatch what had been in Maximus's hands, trying to snag it before blood sloshed over it in its fall. He failed and stood there with it dripping gore.

"The water," said Alik.

Constantine raised an eyebrow as he pulled out the bottle, but he sloshed the water over it. Not all the blood washed off, but enough for him to see a ring of silver, set with green and blue jewels, too large even for Constantine's arm—how suitable. Alik drew a deep breath without looking at the body.

"I need other things, from in there."

Constantine nodded, but his gaze was on the body. "You lured him out with remarkable ease."

Alik laughed—and choked it off, frightening at the wild note he heard. He fought for a moment to steady his voice before he spoke. "Hilarion always said that his reclusiveness would kill him. And so it did. He didn't even know you existed."

He strode off. With the death, they had no choice but swiftness.

The rooms themselves were lit with gray light. Alik flinched. He forced himself to glance about the clutter on tables and cabinets—and flinched again, remembering not the dead madman, but Hilarion. The scrystone glittered there, and more stones, with minor virtues, nothing that Maximus would prize—and Alik forced his gaze away, searching while his thoughts would not leave the question of how long Maximus had waited after Hilarion's death to seize them.

Then, Maximus had not realized he was dead.

Alik's mouth twitched as he glanced over books. They had hustled him off to be a wind-witch quickly enough. They could have done the same to all that Hilarion had kept, and Maximus had taken what he would not prize, without realizing its source.

None of them would help him escape, or he and Hilarion would have long ago left the port. He knew what he wanted, and still looked about.

Once he saw it, the glinting mirror was unmistakable. Alik snatched it and fled to the doorway.

"Maximus didn't need that," Constantine said. "Whatever you intend to do to his spell."

"Maximus," said Alik, "was just going to renew the spell." He walked past the knight. He needed the new moon's light even more than Maximus would have. Some back routes would have kept them from sight, but he set out by the straightest route. He barely looked to see whether pirates could see them as they fled between alleyways; they needed the speed too much.

Constantine sometimes glanced at the crossways, but he did not argue.

Alik felt, with every step, as if a dagger pricked his back. But they reached the Tower of the Stone. The dirt here was hardly packed; it still astounded Alik that he had spied here with the scrystone, or that Hilarion had allowed it. The spells on the tower would not let him in the flesh.

But he had. And Maximus had cast the spells that kept the World's Ways safe here.

He set the mirror on the earth. It could be used to reveal as well as to reverse. And here he needed both—to run Maximus's spell backwards from the mirror, and to reveal the spell that had to be reversed. He drew a deep breath. He had cast both before.

"You might be able to stop the pirates long enough for me to finish the spell," he said, managing to keep his voice steady. "It depends on when they interrupt us."

A ghost of a smile appeared on Constantine's mouth, for only a moment, but he turned to stand watch.

Alik let his breath out. A reversal would not only need his knowledge of the spell, but knowledge of how it worked; he could not do it by rote. Kneeling, he began to sketch out the circle, from the hours when Hilarion had let him test the scrystone, to watch so closely he could know the spell. A protection spell! When he had never quite believed Hilarion that the World's Ways acted like a scrystone.

He plopped the ring in the circle, and put the mirror to reflect it properly. At least, there was no better place to unravel the spell.

Or die.

He finished the circle and stood. For a moment, he contemplated the tower and the walls; then he looked back at the circle. It seemed like threads of light, white and blue and green, extended from the ring to—

Alik stared at it for a minute. Then his mouth curved. No, the thread extended *to* the ring, from the stone. He looked up to see the woven threads through the tower. Maximus had used the stone to twist the very path to the stone. Alik's smile deepened. He did not even need to reverse it, with the threads.

Constantine shifted, but Alik could not turn his attention to see it. He need to see—

A sharp noise, of shattering, had him blink and glance sideways. The mirror lay in a thousand glittering shards, with a rock in their midst. Alik whirled around. Constantine, sword in hand, braced against three pirates, approaching but not in sword's reach.

One was Habrec.

The pirates had not discovered them by chance.

Alik bit his lip but was already reaching for the ring. He had to tuck it under his arm to cast a spell—simple and swift, something used to entertain any crowd. With it in hand, he called, "Constantine! Look at me!"

Constantine whirled around. The pirates lunged, and Alik hurled the spell. Light burst behind Constantine's back. Alik, looking away, caught only glimpses of brilliance, not enough to blind, though plenty enough to make him blink.

That would be seen by every slave and every pirate not already sunk in drunken slumber. And it would hold these three off only for moments.

Constantine ran toward him. Alik, still blinking, scuttled into the tower, hearing Constantine come after, but not daring to take his gaze from a ribbon of white. An explosion of curses from outside told him they had escaped, but Constantine's footsteps slowed behind them.

Alik turned. Constantine looked about the hallway—or, at any rate, turned his face this way and that. Alik was not sure whether he saw anything. He looked down to where blue and white twisted together, reached out to grab Constantine's hand, and despite his flinch, put the hand to the ring.

Constantine blinked, looking about.

"We follow the threads—Maximus must have used the World's Ways to conceal the way in—"

"Does Habrec have one of these?"

Alik flinched. "He would have to."

They went on, not so quickly as they had before, with the ring held awkwardly between them. Still, thought Alik stoutly, this was better than reversing the spell. Only Habrec could follow them now.

Which made him cock his ears for any step.

The thread went on and on, without twisting, or rising. Alik bit his lip. The stone was at the height of the tower, and he could not see how they could reach it without rising, but he also thought they had traveled farther than the tower was wide.

Then, ahead of them, a glow held a thousand such strands, on their own level. And a growl of rage came from behind them.

Constantine whirled, sword in hand, and parried Habrec's blow.

"No!" shouted Alik and threw up his hand, moving through the gestures he had seen Maximus perform. A tangle of lights sprang up between them, and Alik hurled it into Habrec's face.

Constantine must have seen something; he stepped back. Habrec's scream of fury was muffled with distance, though Alik could still see him.

Constantine turned and strode off. Alik, supposing the World's Ways was bright enough for him to see, scrambled after, still holding the ring. Constantine certainly did not hesitate, though once in the doorway, he stopped. Alik scooted around him.

The World's Ways glowed before them. Large enough to fill Alik's cupped hands—larger than the scrystone—rounded smooth, with white and green and blue shifting through its depths every now and again showing little images of far-off things, like the scrystone.

Alik grinned. He should have trusted Hilarion. He tucked the ring under his arm and reached out to take the stone. This might actually work.

A snarl of fury sounded from the doorway. For a moment. Alik stood frozen, wondering how Habrec could have reached here so quickly. Constantine's sword swung to face him; Constantine had never put it up, or even cleaned it, after the last meeting. Alik drew a deep breath and closed his eyes to concentrate on the stone. Swords clashed, and he flinched, and forced his thoughts back to the stone. It could not be too difficult, when Habrec had mastered it. He knew where he wanted, more than he ever had with the scrystone, but finding it and nowhere else was more urgent—

When he opened his eyes again, the tangled ribbons of light showed, not a pirate ship, but Domenic hanging in his chains. He did not even look up at the lights, but shouts came; pirates were watching their prisoner.

Then, he had known his first light spell would rouse them.

"Constantine!" he shouted. Habrec flinched, throwing up his arm to shield his eyes, and Constantine broke off and ran toward him. Moments later, Habrec snarled and ran after. Alik wished he had a light spell, but—no matter. He jumped through. Constantine leapt after him, and Habrec after him. Constantine turned with a snarl as fierce as Habrec's and rejoined the fight, standing braced before Dominic without yielding an inch.

Alik shoved both stone and ring into a niche in the wall and ran. They did not keep the keys far off.

He stepped through the doorway into the building. The key ring hung the wall, he could see it, but a pirate stood between him and it, and though his hand was steady, he was reaching for his sword. Alik yanked his knife and stabbed. The pirate's shout would draw more, but the spewing blood gave him a moment to fly by and snatch the keys, as the pirate's hand leapt to staunch the wound.

"You cursed—"

Alik stabbed again. The pirate parried the blow. Not easily—but he was not drunk enough to be easy prey. Alik lunged, and the knife struck into his throat. The knife drove too deeply for Alik to pull out, but the gurgle in the pirate's throat said he had stopped him well enough.

At the price of not being able to stop another—Alik ran. No time to think, even—especially—when he heard the pirate thud to the floor.

Habrec and Constantine fought furiously, blocking the walkway. Alik snagged the World's Ways and, his back firmly against the wall, away from the fall to the waters, bent his attention on it again. Easy this time to see what he wanted—he leapt through a tangle to drop beside Domenic and kneel to unlock the chains.

With the key clicking in the lock, Domenic stirred a little and watched Alik with unreadable eyes. The chains fell free, and Domenic tried to push off the ground, steadying himself on Alik's arm.

Swords flashing in their hands, pirates stormed out the doorway behind Habrec where—Alik pushed Domenic's hand to the wall and seized the World's Ways. As if he could save them. He had thought he had realized that he might not, but failure was sour in his mouth. Habrec would just jump through any tangle he made. Any attempt to distract him would take out Constantine as well. He no longer had his knife. Even if he could find Domenic a sword, and Domenic could fight, they would have only two against—

For a moment, Alik could not breathe. Then he closed his eyes and concentrated again. He heard Domenic move and opened his own eyes. A smooth, mirror-like floor spread through the tangle. He leapt without looking for more, went sprawling, and scrambled away on hands and knees without daring to rise, or even to look up from the pale marble; it would take too much time. He did not know how he held onto the World's Ways, but he heard Domenic follow.

Moments later, Constantine sprang after. Habrec and the pirates roared, and surged through.

Inside the hall, glittering with mirrors and candles, scores of swords sprang up, encircling Constantine and the pirates, engulfing Domenic and Alik. Constantine, facing Habrec, was firmly drawn back by the royal guard. Habrec and the pirates turned back.

Ready to laugh, Alik clutched the World's Ways and dismissed the tangle, leaving him clutching an uncommon-looking stone that showed no signs of magic and fighting down laughter. Not that many looked at him, with the pirates standing before the guard, and the courtiers who, by law, had wear swords at court.

He looked from the slaughter. He himself had killed this hour. He had killed, to tell the truth, more before it. After the way this started—

The air did not smell of salt and sea. Something of dust, but that was what he himself had brought. The smell of blood joined that of burning candle wax. He studied the floor even as the clash of steel and other battle sounds ended, until men spoke of being rid of the bodies.

A grizzled knight spoke to Constantine and Domenic.

Domenic said, "I can stand long enough for a royal audience."

He sounded dazed, as if Alik knew any place other than the royal palace where he could bring swords to bear. Alik smiled a little. He had. . . he had. . . he looked into the depths of the World's Ways, and his smile faded as the thought of all that happened bore down on him.

"And you, Alik?" Constantine looked down at him.

Alik blinked.

"Can you stand long enough for a royal audience?"

A royal audience? Alik pondered a moment. This one, he guessed—he hoped—would be more pleasant than his first. Holding the stone against himself with one hand, he pushed himself up with the other. Constantine's hand came out to steady him. A moment later, Constantine withdrew it, but he did not step away.

The grizzled knight looked at the World's Ways but did not speak, only spread his hand toward the great golden doors, arrayed with stars and suns and moons, with swords and sheaves of wheat, with a crown presiding over all.

It looked more impressive than it had the last time, thought Alik. And it slid silently open before them.

Behind it, courtiers still hurried through doors and across the floor, to position themselves to either side of the throne. Many were still in disarray, straightening badges and robes of office as they took their places. King Petros himself had not quite the august attire that Alik remembered.

Constantine and Domenic bowed. Alik tried one as well; the stone made it clumsy. He blinked. He felt more tired than he ever had before in his life.

"What is the meaning of this?" said King Petros, regally.

"It means that the pirates would not have sailed to Kingsport." Alik lifted the World's Ways. "Now they will not sail anywhere at all."

Constantine reached out and firmly took the stone from his hands. Alik blinked at him. Constantine handed Domenic it and reached out to pick up Alik.

Like a baby, thought Alik. He could hear voices, and the rumble of speech in Constantine's chest, but he made out only one phrase: "My father's house."

Which still made no sense when he found himself with his face in a pillow. A full, white pillow. Swathes of white surrounded him. He even wore some kind of white tunic, and he no longer smelled of dust. He sat up.

Curtains surrounded the bed—pale embroidered deer, birds, and rabbits gamboled in riots of flowers and trees—but one curtain had been pulled back to show a white-washed room. A window showed a cityscape, in broad day, with the sun beating down on it. By the door, there stood a boy wearing a white robe with blue stripes about the wrist and throat.

The boy gasped and ran out. "He's awake, he's awake," and footsteps echoed in the corridor outside, until distance muffled the sounds. Alik scrambled from bed and went to the window.

A garden spread a floor below, filled with trees and sweet-smelling roses. Past the wall, gracious buildings spread, the highest among them the royal castle. Even from here, he could see the bustle about it.

A snort came from the doorway. A lean, grizzled man, who wore robes like the boy's, looked him up and down.

"I told them you were nothing more than tired—and you have confirmed my judgment—but you must nonetheless submit to examination."

Alik eyed him warily but went back to the bed. Slitting his throat in the night would have been easy enough. They did not mean him that ill.

The man inspected him minutely, with spells he had never seen before. Rosalba had cast some like them, but not very like.

Minutes inched by, and then the man called for menservants to attend Alik.

Once they had combed his hair out and dressed him in royal blue and white, they bustled him off. Alik found himself in a long hall. Curtained windows stood to one hand, a carpet figured with flowers lay underfoot—a carpet as fine as anything the pirates had ever seized, and this one was not tracked with red dust—and mirrors, to the other hand. In the shadowy light, Alik took a dubious look at himself. The only thing that distinguished him from a pirate was that the clothing fit. And, he had to admit, the colors did not clash, or look uncomely on him.

"Ah, my young guest stirs."

The man walking down the hall wore robes of office in deep red. His hair was grizzled, but his eyes were a familiar shade of amber. The servant bowed, and the man dismissed him with a wave of his hand, not looking from Alik. The corners of his mouth quirked, causing wrinkles beside his eyes, and he bowed.

Alik, vaguely remembering what he had seen at court, bowed back.

"Come, Master Alik. In return for my son's life, I may offer you—breakfast. But then His Majesty requires your presence at the castle. They may not start without you."

Alik followed him into a room, and sat to eat. He recognized most of the dishes—he thought—at least what they were made of—but if the pirates had cooks among their captives, they still had no meals like this.

He looked up from a dish of fruit and porridge. "But—the castle—they were so busy—"

The man lifted an eyebrow. "They can ready themselves for the attack. My son and Sir Domenic can instruct them all in what they know of their encampment. But only one wizard can let them through."

The World's Ways could not be too hard to master. Not when Habrec, no wizard, had mastered it. Not when one badly trained young wizard had mastered it swiftly with no more knowledge than how to use a scrystone. . . . Alik smiled in silence and dug into the meal.

Not an hour later, the journey to the castle carried out by carriage, Alik stood before the king for a third time. The World's Ways gleamed on the table as King Petros gravely told him that on Sir Constantine's advice, they would land the forces on the beach, by the camp.

"And soon." King Petros looked, brooding, on the stone. "We have set watch for any ships, and any wind-witching, but the more pirates we catch there, the better."

Alik nodded.

"You, of course, will remain here, until word is sent that the gate should reopen, as you tried to send word of their attack. We can not risk you, you need to rest, and there is no need, really, for you to ever return."

"There are wizards there," said Alik brightly. "With—" He waved a hand. "All sorts of magical things, all the pirates' loot. My master taught me much of it." He glanced sideways. "I could help keep it innocuous. And some of it, my master wanted to be mine, after he died."

Ministers looked dismayed. Constantine and Domenic exchanged wry glances.

The king snorted. "You are a bold one."

"While I lived among the pirates, Your Majesty, nothing could be mine without my grabbing with both hands." He shrugged. "As I grabbed the World's Ways, and the lives of your knights, from the hands of the pirates."

King Petros laughed. "Your aid in dealing with such wizardry will inspire gratitude—after the battle."

Alik grinned and turned to the World's Ways. "Tell me where, and I will open the gates."

Also by Mary Catelli

Curses And Wonders
Dragon Slayer
Eyes of the Sorceress
Fever and Snow
Mermaids' Song
Sword and Shadow
The Book of Bone
Witch-Prince Ways
Dragonfire and Time
Enchantments And Dragons
Jewel of the Tiger
Over the Sea, To Me
The Dragon's Cottage
The Maze, the Manor, and the Unicorn
The White Menagerie
A Diabolical Bargain
Madeleine and the Mists
Magic And Secrets
The Lion and the Library
The Princess Goes Into The Forest
The Wolf and the Ward
The Witch-Child and the Scarlet Fleet
Treachery And Spells
Winter's Curse
Crow Curse
Free Passage
Isabelle and the Siren
Journeys And Wizardry
Lifestone

Magic of the Lost God
Never Comment On A Likeness
One Name
The Drunken Mermaids
The Turtle in the Sea of Sand
Were I You
Where There Is Smoke

www.ingramcontent.com/pod-product-compliance
Lightning Source LLC
Chambersburg PA
CBHW020646130626
46552CB00003B/1417